Jennifer Hunter is a retired mediator who lives in south-eastern Australia. She enjoys working in the garden and growing her own vegetables, baking chocolate desserts, singing pineal tones, and reading. This publication is her first attempt at a little novel and is loosely based upon her spiritual beliefs and experiences.

This book is dedicated to my grandchildren—Rhys, Maddison, Nadim, Adia, Harrison, and Tuscany—whose efforts to raise the Earth's vibration I look forward to witnessing, either during this life or the life to come.

Jennifer Hunter

LITTLE SOUL

AUSTIN MACAULEY PUBLISHERS™

LONDON • CAMBRIDGE • NEW YORK • SHARJAH

A CIP catalogue record for this title is available from the British Library.

ISBN 9781035847709 (Paperback)
ISBN 9781035847716 (ePub e-book)

www.austinmacauley.com

First Published 2024
Austin Macauley Publishers Ltd®
1 Canada Square
Canary Wharf
London
E14 5AA

Many thanks for all the assistance given by the staff of
Austin Macauley

Table of Contents

What's Earth?

There was once a little soul who lived with many other souls inside the beautiful Light of the Creator. Little Soul was very happy with his life and never thought about living anywhere else. The Creator was very loving, and His Light was always comforting, so Little Soul couldn't imagine being in any other place.

Little Soul spent many years watching other souls coming and going, but he never gave much thought as to where they might be going or what they might be doing. He thought his life was perfect, and it was.

Then one day, as Little Soul was watching another soul returning to the Creator's Light, he noticed a group of souls greeting the returning one, and they appeared to be celebrating something. Little Soul felt curious for the first time in his life, and he decided to ask one of the old souls what was happening.

"Old Soul, I saw you and the others looking very happy as you greeted the returning soul, and I was wondering if you were celebrating something special."

"Well, yes, we were," replied the old soul. "Our friend just returned from Earth after many years, and we were welcoming him back home."

"What's Earth?" asked Little Soul.

"Earth is a place where souls can go to experience something special. It's like a school where you learn many new and interesting things. You can stay either for a short time or for many years. Then you return to the Creator's Light before deciding if you wish to do something else."

"What kind of new things do you learn?" Little Soul asked.

"Would you like to see a soul who has recently travelled to Earth, Little Soul? It can be arranged for you to watch the soul begin his life on Earth and see some of his many adventures if you would be interested."

Little Soul was now really curious and he answered excitedly, "Yes, I would!"

Old Soul took Little Soul aside and instructed him to watch very carefully and quietly as the soul began his new life on Earth. As Little Soul looked down, he suddenly saw something strange and rather wonderful.

"What are those things in that group?" he asked in a whispery voice.

"Those are people," replied Old Soul. "They are waiting to welcome the soul to Earth. The one in the bed will be his mother, and the one standing at her side will be his father. They will take care of the soul while he is on Earth. The others are there to assist the soul's arrival into his new life."

Little Soul was just about to whisper another question when suddenly he heard a little noise and saw another person—a tiny one—being placed into the arms of the mother. He forgot his first question, and almost forgot to use his whispery voice for his next question, which was: "What is that little thing in the mother's arms? It's so small."

"That's the soul," replied Old Soul. "He will be in that body while he is on Earth."

"But he's so tiny compared to the others," said Little Soul.

"He'll grow bigger over the years," replied Old Soul.

"What are years?"

"They are a way of measuring time on Earth, Little Soul. Things are different there and people aren't able to see everything all at once. Years are a measurement of the passage of time. People get older each year and experience different things each year. When they have learned enough, or have completed their life's purpose, then their body dies and their soul returns to the Creator."

"What's 'life purpose'?" asked Little Soul.

"Souls spend time on Earth for a reason," replied Old Soul. "They go there to help make it a better place."

"How do they do that?" asked Little Soul.

"They go there with the Creator's love and, when they arrive, they are born with special gifts. Some can paint beautiful pictures, some can sing beautiful songs, some can teach others, and some are there to show great kindness. Their gifts are endless and all of them are important."

While Little Soul was busy asking so many questions, the first year of the baby's life had passed, and the little one was now just starting to take his first steps. Little Soul noticed the beaming smiles on the faces of the baby's mother and father as they encouraged their child to walk from one to the other. "They seem to really love the baby," said Little Soul.

"Yes," replied Old Soul. "Parents on Earth love their children just as the Creator loves us."

Food, School, Work, Pain

Little Soul continued to watch the family as they sat down to eat a meal. "What are they doing now?" he asked.

"They're eating food. That's what people on Earth do to keep their bodies going," explained Old Soul.

"Where does the food come from?" asked Little Soul.

"There are places on Earth where plants are grown," replied Old Soul, "and there are other places where animals are raised for meat."

"Could I see some of these places, Old Soul?"

"Certainly, Little Soul. Come with me and look down over here."

Little Soul gasped as he looked at a group of cows grazing in a field. "Do people eat these beautiful things?"

"Some people do," replied Old Soul. "Others prefer to eat only the plants."

"I don't think I could eat anything," said Little Soul. "Everything is too beautiful to disturb and, besides, eating looks like too much work."

Old Soul chuckled. "People don't think of eating as work. In fact, most of them enjoy eating, and some of them enjoy it so much that they actually eat more than they need."

Little Soul continued with his questions and, when he next looked down at the baby, it was no longer a baby, but a little boy ready for his first day at school. "He has grown so much!" exclaimed Little Soul. "What is he doing now?"

"He and his mother are walking to school. It's his first day and he's very excited about meeting his teacher and making new friends," explained Old Soul.

"What will he do at school?" asked Little Soul.

"He will learn to do many new things that humans need to know how to do, such as how to read and write. He will also be able to paint pictures, sing songs and play with his friends," replied Old Soul.

Little Soul had so many questions about Earth school that, when he looked down again, the boy was no longer little but was now as tall as his father. He was at some kind of celebration and his father and mother looked very proud and happy. "What's happening now?" Little Soul asked.

"The boy has just finished an important part of his schooling and is at a ceremony that people on Earth have when their children reach this stage in their lives. They're usually about eighteen years of age. It is now time for them to decide whether to go to work to earn a living, or continue to study for several more years to prepare for some particular type of work which they feel they would like to do."

"Why do people have to work?" Little Soul asked.

"That's the way they earn money to buy food to eat and houses for shelter," replied Old Soul.

"Life is so difficult on Earth," said Little Soul. "In the Creator's Light, we never have to worry about anything. I don't understand why anyone would want to live on Earth."

"It is a very special thing for a soul to go to Earth," explained Old Soul. "Earth experiences are like a school for souls. They learn about many things, especially about love, and how it feels to give and to receive love. And they learn about this in a most extraordinary way because sometimes they experience not being loving and not being loved by others, and their pain helps them return to love."

"What is pain?" asked Little Soul.

"There are different kinds of pain," answered Old Soul. "One is physical and is felt by the body when a person is sick or injured. The other is a feeling people get inside when their bodies are not hurting but they feel sad about something. This sad pain is a very special pain because it often helps them to remember the Creator, and remembering the Creator often leads them back to happiness."

"Why do they need to remember the Creator?" asked Little Soul. "How could they ever forget Him in the first place?"

"Ah, that's the whole idea of coming to Earth, Little Soul. Your memory of the Creator's Light is removed temporarily when you enter Earth. This allows you to have special experiences with your family and others and, also, to learn many valuable lessons while you are there. This helps you and it helps the Earth."

"How can it help the Earth? What kind of lessons would do this?" Little Soul asked.

"A soul comes to Earth with a special purpose, but then does not always remember what that purpose is, and often goes through many experiences trying to discover why he or she is on Earth. When the person finally figures out what their purpose is, and lives life in a way to realise this purpose, it helps to raise the spiritual vibration of Earth," explained Old Soul.

"I don't understand. Why does Earth's vibration raise?" asked Little Soul.

"A person's life purpose involves service either to Earth or to others, and service is connected to love, so it is this love which raises the vibration," replied Old Soul.

"Okay, I think I understand but I need to think about this some more," said Little Soul. "Maybe it would help if I could see what this boy I have been watching does with his life."

"Alright, Little Soul, let's see where he is now. Ah—he has just discovered his life's purpose and a lot younger than most people! The young man has decided that he wants to help others less fortunate than himself and has travelled to a place in a country far away from his home to do this. It is so exciting. Look!"

Little Soul looked down and saw that the boy was now a man, and that he had left his father and mother and was in a strange land. He was surrounded by many people of a different colour and they looked very thin and hungry. The young man was offering them food and water and was comforting those who looked sick or sad. Occasionally he turned away to wipe tears from his eyes.

"What has happened to these people, Old Soul? Why are they so hungry and sad?"

"There have been many troubles in their land, Little Soul. There hasn't been rain for a long time so they have been unable to grow food to eat. There have also been some wars near their homes and they have had to leave so their families would be safe."

"What are wars?" asked Little Soul.

"Sometimes people have so much difficulty remembering the Creator that they forget about love entirely, and then they become very unhappy," explained Old Soul. "They don't realise that their unhappiness is because they have forgotten about love, and they start to blame others for all the misery in their lives. Instead of sharing love, they begin to share their misery and do things that will make others miserable, too. They begin to want things that other people have and will fight to take these things. They may take others' money and possessions, and sometimes they even take their homes and land. They think that having what others own will make them happy, but what they are really looking for is love. They have simply forgotten about the Creator and His love which is always available to everyone."

"Could I see a war?" asked Little Soul.

"Yes, but it might upset you," replied Old Soul. "Have a look down there."

Little Soul gasped. There were men riding inside strange things that looked like huge boxes, and others were carrying all sorts of odd objects in their hands. These men were hurting and even killing each other. "How can they do that?" asked Little Soul. "Earth is a terrible place! I could never go there!"

"Yes, it does look terrible," Old Soul replied, "but the lessons these people will learn in this life are very precious. When they return to the Creator, they will be comforted, and they will review all the things they have learned from their earthly experience. They will be amazed that they could so easily forget about the Creator and their special life purpose. And most of them will decide to take on another body and experience another existence somewhere. And, once again, they will express their intention to remember the Creator and their life purpose, but again this may be difficult. Also, as before, many valuable lessons will be gained, and remembering love will further increase the spiritual vibration of Earth."

"Could we go back and see how the young man is doing, Old Soul?"

"Of course, Little Soul. But you will see that he is quite a bit older now, and many new things have happened in his life."

Love

Little Soul looked down and was surprised at what he saw. The young man was not only older, but he was with a woman and two small children. The woman had a dark-coloured skin like the people the young man had been helping when Little Soul had seen him last, but the man and the woman were now back in the country where Little Soul had first seen this man enter Earth.

"What happened?" Little Soul asked.

"Our young man got married and now has a son and a daughter of his own," replied Old Soul. "He has brought his wife back to study so she can become a doctor and go back to help her people. That is her life purpose, and the man she married is helping her to realise this purpose."

"Okay, I feel a little better now," said Little Soul. "I guess Earth isn't all bad."

"Earth isn't bad at all," replied Old Soul. "It's the perfect place to learn many important lessons about love. You can't really appreciate love until you experience its absence, so all experiences are important and necessary, even those that are painful."

Little Soul continued to ask questions about life on Earth, purpose, love, and everything else he could think of. Old Soul patiently answered each question and showed Little Soul many Earth scenes to help him understand. Then he said, "Little Soul, look quickly. There is a very special event happening that you might want to see."

Little Soul looked down. What he saw was a very old man lying in a bed with people all around him. "Who is that man?" Little Soul asked.

"That is the man we were watching earlier, Little Soul. He is now at the end of his life on Earth, and his family have gathered around to say 'good-bye' to him."

"Some of them have tears in their eyes," Little Soul observed. "Why are they sad?"

"What you are seeing isn't really sadness, Little Soul. It's love. His family and friends will miss the man when he leaves his body behind on Earth, but they know that the most important part of him—his soul—will continue, and they are happy that he is soon to be released to return to the Light of the Creator. They are also grateful that they had so many years with this special man, for he lived to be ninety-five, and he did many wonderful things to help many people."

"So, he helped to raise the spiritual vibration of Earth?" asked Little Soul.

"Definitely," replied Old Soul.

"Is there anything else I should see now?"

"Yes, there is, Little Soul. Have a look over here at this young couple. You might find them quite interesting."

Little Soul looked down once more and saw a young man with a young woman, and they looked so happy that they seemed to glow. "What makes them look like that?" asked Little Soul, curiously. "Has some special thing happened to them?"

"Why, yes," replied Old Soul. "They have fallen deeply in love with each other, and they have decided it is time to share all that love with a child."

"Gee, they certainly must love each other very much," said Little Soul. "I can actually feel the love from here."

"You know, Little Soul, if you are feeling love pulling you towards Earth, you are free to go there," said Old Soul. "Life might not always be easy for you, but you would certainly learn many exciting things, and you would never be alone, even if you were to feel that way sometimes. There are so many wonderful souls on Earth that you would surely feel the love connection much of the time. And that young couple you just saw would be the most wonderful parents."

"Yes!" exclaimed Little Soul. "I would like to go to Earth! I want to give love. I want that to be my life's purpose. I want to love everybody!"

And with that, Little Soul hurried to begin his life on Earth. Before he got too far away, he asked Old Soul, "Will I be a boy or a girl?"

Old Soul smiled and said, "You decide."

Michael's Arrival and First Year

Today was Little Soul's birthday! It wasn't his first or second birthday, or any other birthday with a number. It was actually the day he was being born, and he was both nervous and excited.

For the past nine months, Little Soul had been floating around happily in his mother's womb, but during the past few weeks, he had been growing so fast that his womb home had started to feel somewhat cramped. Little Soul had begun to think that a bit more space for his very active arms and legs would be rather nice.

Now Little Soul began to feel really cramped as he was being pushed out of the womb for his birth into Earth life. He began to feel a little panicky until, suddenly, Little Soul heard the calm voice of his friend, Old Soul. "Don't worry, Little Soul. You might feel a little uncomfortable now but you will be fine when you are born. Everything will be very different but you will soon love it. I will visit you from time to time to see how you are doing."

And then it happened! Little Soul made it out of the birth canal and found himself being gently held by a lady in white. He took his first breath and let out a great cry, which seemed to make her very happy. She then handed Little Soul to someone lying in a bed, a lady whom he recognised as the one he had chosen to be his mother. Standing next to her bed was the man who was his father. Little Soul was very excited, but suddenly he realised that he couldn't communicate with these people to let them know he had chosen them. All he could do was look deeply into their eyes. Fortunately, his look seemed to make them very happy, and their eyes filled with tears of joy. Little Soul knew that it was joy because he could feel it when they looked at him.

"Have you chosen a name for your son?" asked the lady in white, who was a midwife.

"Oh, yes," answered Little Soul's mother. "We have chosen the name Michael."

"Wow," thought Little Soul. "I'm a boy and my name is Michael. I wish I could tell Old Soul."

"I'm right here beside you," said Old Soul. "You have been given a fine name, Michael. You actually share that name with an archangel. You need to rest now, so just close your eyes and have a little sleep."

Michael slept peacefully, smiling in his sleep as Old Soul sang him a lullaby. His parents looked at him in amazement. "Look, he's smiling," exclaimed Michael's mother. "I wonder what he's dreaming about."

Tiny Michael was smiling because he wasn't actually present in his body. While his little body slept, his spirit was visiting with Old Soul. He had a lot of questions to ask and concerns to share with his old friend, even though he hadn't even been on Earth for quite an hour.

"Old Soul, I can't talk to my new parents," Michael said. "I have all these thoughts but I just can't get them out of my mouth. What am I to do? Will my parents still want me when they discover that I am unable to speak?"

Old Soul gave a hearty laugh and replied, "You don't have to worry about any of that. You are not expected to talk just yet. That will take a bit of time. Meanwhile, whenever you need to communicate, you will make crying sounds which will vary according to what, and how urgent, your needs are. Your parents will pick you up, comfort you, feed you, cuddle you, change you, or do whatever else might be needed to make you comfortable."

"What do you mean when you say that they will 'change' me? I just got here. What is it about me that needs to be changed?"

Old Soul laughed again. He so enjoyed his conversations with little Michael. "Well, Michael, on Earth you will find that you do not have the same abilities that you had when you lived in the Light of the Creator. You will develop abilities and talents over time, so don't worry. Earth parents expect their children to arrive in a helpless state, and they take great delight in watching them develop gradually. For the time being, you will need to adjust to having your parents do everything for you—feeding you, carrying you everywhere, and changing your clothes, especially the nappies that you will wear to collect the waste produced whenever you are fed."

"You've got to be kidding!" Little Soul exclaimed. "I didn't realise that I volunteered for THIS! Why didn't you tell me?"

"I don't think you would have believed me," replied Old Soul. "Trust me, you will get used to all this and you will even be happy. The love that you and your parents will share will be beautiful. Meanwhile, I will continue to visit you off and on for a few years to see how you are doing. Now you must wake up so your mother can feed you her milk so you will be a strong, healthy baby. It is an experience that you will soon grow to love. Good-bye for now, Michael."

Michael awoke suddenly and was so hungry that his little tummy hurt. He cried very loudly and his mother picked him up and placed him on her breast. Michael drank until he was full and comfortable. His mother smiled and talked to him for a while, and Michael enjoyed the soothing tone of her voice. He just wished that he could tell her so many things, but that would have to wait—for how long Michael had no idea.

Time passed and gradually Michael stayed awake for longer periods of time. He was still unable to talk, but now he made little cooing and babbling sounds. They made no sense whatsoever, but his mother and father seemed to love hearing them so much that Michael put his best efforts into making them. Now he was even able to smile back at his parents who seemed absolutely thrilled whenever this happened.

One day, as he was kicking his legs on his special soft blanket on the floor, Michael suddenly discovered that he could roll over. His mother was delighted! A few weeks after that, Michael was able to scoot around a bit on the blanket. His parents were so pleased. "Gee, it certainly doesn't take much to make Mum and Dad happy," Michael thought. "If only I could show them what I was like before I came to Earth. That would really make them excited!"

Shortly after mastering the rolling and scooting, Michael was able to pull himself up onto his hands and knees, and he began to crawl. "This is more like it," he thought. "Now I can go everywhere!" His parents were so proud of their baby that you would have thought Michael was magical if you heard the way they described his accomplishments.

Another day, Old Soul came to visit Michel again. "It's good to see that you are getting around so well, Michael. Soon you will move around with even more ease, and you will be able to reach things with less effort. It's so lovely to see your smile. I told you you'd be happy!"

"It's really not so bad now, Old Soul. My mother and father are really nice. If I have to live on Earth for a while, I am very lucky to have them. I think they love me as much as the Creator does."

"I'm happy that you are making such a wonderful adjustment, Michael. Everyone doesn't, you know. Some babies arrive with great challenges. You, too, will have your challenges, but they will come later. Meanwhile, please remember that you will always be loved by your parents and the Creator during both good times and bad." Old Soul smiled at Michael and disappeared once again.

One day, as Michel was pulling himself up so he could cling to a chair, he spied his favourite teddy bear on the couch. Michael held onto the chair as he took little steps towards the couch and, when he reached the edge of the chair, without thinking, he took a few little steps on his own! Then he sat down with a 'plop.' Michael's mum saw him take those first steps and became very excited. She rushed over to Michael, helped him stand up, and held his little hand until he reached the couch and grabbed the teddy bear. "Well done, Michael," she said. "Soon you will be walking around all the time on your own." Then she gave him a big kiss.

A few weeks later it was little Michael's first Earth birthday—the one with the number 1! His mother made him a cake that looked a little like his favourite teddy bear. She put one candle in the middle of it and lit it with a match, while Michael's father took photos with a camera. They sang 'Happy Birthday,' blew out the candle for Michael, and then cut him the biggest piece of cake he had ever seen. It was delicious. Michael ate it with his little hands and made a big mess, but his parents just smiled proudly. He certainly would have had a tummy ache if most of the cake hadn't ended up on the floor on its way to his mouth.

The Challenge Appears and School at Last!

Before he knew it, another two years had passed, and Michael was just about to turn three. His first three years had been very happy ones for Michael and his parents, but friends and other members of the family had begun to share their concerns about Michael's progress.

"He really should be talking by now," several family friends said. "Perhaps you should have a chat with your doctor."

Michael's parents were upset whenever these comments were made, but they took him for a check-up and asked the doctor about his progress. "I think we'll have his hearing tested," the doctor said.

The hearing test was completed and it seemed that little Michael could hear just fine. Then the doctor said, "I notice that Michael doesn't seem to want to look at me. Is he like this with other people?"

"Well, he looks at us and he looks at his grandparents, but he does seem to avoid looking directly at most people. We think he might be a bit shy."

"What does Michael do when he plays?" asked the doctor.

"Well, he's quite active and loves to run around, especially outdoors, and he can jump on his little trampoline for hours! When he's tired, he loves to hug his teddy bear. When he plays with his blocks and trucks, he puts them into the straightest lines you ever saw!" said Michael's mother.

The doctor was silent for a moment and then asked, "Have you ever heard or read anything about autism?"

Michael's parents looked at each other in a worried way and asked the doctor at the same time, "You don't think Michael is autistic, do you?"

"Well, I'm not absolutely certain. I'll make arrangements for someone to observe him and then we'll see what they have to say."

A few days later a lady named Rosie came to visit Michael in his home and watched him as he played. When Michael ran outside, Rosie joined him and talked to him for a while. She told Michael that he would be coming to see her the next week and that they could play some more. When that day arrived, she joined Michael in a lot of activities—puzzles, blocks, cars, flash cards, drawing, and some attempts at conversation. Michael really didn't understand what was going on, but he picked up all the objects that were offered to him and organised them in his very special way. He didn't have a lot of words in his vocabulary to help him take part in the conversation properly, so Michael just tried to send out his best thoughts. It was a great relief when his mum and dad were allowed to leave with him and return home. Michael always felt much more comfortable and happy in his own home environment.

Michael's parents were soon called back to see Rosie. "Thank you for coming to discuss the results of Michael's tests," she said to them. "It appears that Michael is indeed autistic, although not too severely. We'll put you into contact with people who can help you with the skills you will need to help Michael develop his speech and to communicate more effectively in other ways."

And so Michael's journey within the official world of autism began. His parents got him the help he needed, and gradually Michael learned lots of new things. His speech improved with help from a special therapist, and he was able to communicate much better. His occasional tantrums—which drew many looks of disapproval when out in public—soon disappeared, as Michael was now able to express his needs more readily. He could now verbally let his parents know when he had spent enough time outside his much-loved home.

When Michael was three-and-a-half, the family was blessed with the arrival of another child—a little girl named Claire. Claire was too small to play with Michael so he didn't have much to do with her during her first few months. Then, when she began to crawl, Claire began to follow him around and Michael felt a lot of love coming from such a tiny person. It was so strong that Michael couldn't help but return Claire's love, even though people observing them couldn't always see it.

One day Old Soul came for another visit while Michael was having an afternoon nap. He didn't usually have naps, but little Claire was teething and had cried so loudly that Michael woke up in the middle of the night. He couldn't get back to sleep which made him very tired and cranky the next day.

"Hello, Michael!" said Old Soul. "It's nice to see you growing so well. And you have a little sister! So much has happened in your life and you are having so many new adventures."

"Yes, I am," replied Michael. "I never could have imagined all this while living in the Light of the Creator. Some things are really challenging, but I am glad that I decided to come to Earth. I wish I could talk to my sister. I sometimes feel that she is trying to tell me things but without words."

"She IS communicating with you, Michael. She is sharing the most important message of all—the message of love. If you stay next to her long enough you will definitely be able to feel it. She actually wanted to come to Earth to be your sister. Years from now, when you both return to the Creator, you will discuss your earthly adventures, but for now you will have to settle for her little gurgles of pleasure when you are around."

"Did she really want to be my sister? I seem to be a challenging person for so many people."

"Yes, she really chose you. And, yes, you do present challenges, but you also offer gifts, and these will soon be obvious to those who love you. We'll talk more about this another time. For now, you need to wake up and be your challenging self." And with that, Old Soul disappeared, and Michael opened his eyes and jumped out of bed.

Before he knew it, another two years had passed and Michael was now five years old. His parents wanted to enrol him in the local kindergarten, so they decided to visit the school and discuss Michael's needs and challenges. "We'd be happy to have Michael at our school, but you will need to take him to the doctor and put him on proper medication first so he will be happier and easier to manage," the principal had said.

His parents were disappointed, as they didn't think that Michael needed to be medicated. He was very active, but no more active than lots of other little boys. Michael often played a little differently than other children, but he was a happy little boy and had never hurt anyone.

Michael's parents then made two very important decisions. First, they decided to home school Michael. And then they decided to move to another town—one where they both had grown up and, as young humans often do, had insisted that they would never live in again! Both sets of their parents still lived in this town and they all loved Michael dearly. And they were all very happy to help with Michael's schooling. Michael's father's parents had been teachers. Grandma Ann had taught children in primary school, and Grandpa Bill had taught music, mostly the piano and organ. Michael's mother's parents—Grandma Jan and Grandpa Jack—had run a landscaping business and now, in their retirement, they grew their own flowers and vegetables. All these people had special skills that would change little Michael's life in ways that no one could have ever imagined.

And so the move was made, and young Michael thrived. One set of his grandparents introduced him to the world of plants, which Michael immediately loved. The other grandparents taught Michael other things. Grandma Ann gradually taught him to read, and Grandpa Bill began to teach Michael the piano, only to discover that Michael was already able to play the piano and could play back everything he heard. Everyone was amazed and felt so blessed to have this special little boy in the family.

Michael continued to progress over the next few years, and soon the time came for Claire to start school. When it became obvious to Michael that his sister was going to school every day while he stayed at home, Michael told his parents that he also wanted to go to school. He loved learning the many things that his grandparents were teaching him, but he really wanted to go to school with Claire.

Michael's parents remembered the conversation with the principal of the first school and were a bit anxious about their son's decision. They went to Claire's school and were told, to their delight, that Michael would be welcome at their school, and they were asked to bring him to determine what class he should be in and what special help he might need. Michael's parents were overjoyed, as they thought it was important for Michael to spend time with other children.

And so Michael's school life began. On the night before his very first day of school, Old Soul came for a visit. "Well, Michael," he said, "it's so wonderful to see you progressing in life. You're eight years old now and our little chats will become fewer and further apart. Just remember, Michael, you can talk to me anytime in your thoughts and I will answer in your thoughts. Just continue to pay attention to your feelings. You have always done that so well."

Michael made good progress in school. His mother and Grandma Ann continued to tutor him at home, and they also took turns visiting the school and helping Michael whenever he needed it. As it turned out, to everyone's surprise, Michael loved numbers and was gifted in mathematics. His teacher was kind and patient and praised Michael's efforts, and he loved her very much.

Michael made friends at school. The kids knew he was a little different because the teacher had prepared them before his arrival. They invited him to play at recess and sometimes he happily joined them. At other times he preferred to be by himself, so they left him alone with his thoughts.

The school took a great deal of interest in Michael and very carefully chose his teacher every year. Each teacher was eager to help Michael, and he enjoyed most of his school experience. His mother and grandmother continued taking turns coming to the school to assist him when this was needed. Each year this became less and less until it was no longer necessary when he entered Year 6.

Michael finished primary school and then began high school, where he had different teachers for the different subjects which he was studying. When his parents visited the school to talk to the principal about Michael, the principal assured them that family members would always be welcome and that there was also a special mentoring program for Michael. A young man would be available on certain days to assist Michael and to make sure that he was understanding the requirements of his classes. He would also be available after school, and Michael could talk to him about anything that was on his mind. This young man—whose name was Joseph—had an autistic brother. Joseph had helped his brother as they were growing up, and he had decided that he wanted to do something that would help other autistic children. Michael connected with Joseph straight away, and they had a special bond. Joseph could tell when Michael was confused in class and he helped him with any difficulties.

Joseph mentored Michael for his first two years of high school, after which Michael was able to manage on his own. He helped keep Michael organised for assignments and tests. Joseph also encouraged Michael to try out a few sports. Michael didn't like any kind of ball sports, but he had always loved swimming, and easily made it onto the high school swimming team. Michael seemed to have been born knowing how to swim. The first time his parents had taken him to the local pool for lessons as a young boy, Michael had amazed everyone by jumping into the pool and swimming all the way to the other side. He had absolutely no fear of the water. Now Michael won many competitions on the high school swimming team and even won a trophy for the school's trophy cabinet!

Michael graduated from high school and his parents and sister were so proud! Claire was always talking about her future plans to attend university when she finished high school. It was her dream to become a teacher for children with special needs. Their parents wondered if Michael had any desires for the future that would require further study. "Would you like to go to university, Michael?" they asked.

"No!" Michael replied. "I want to start a plant nursery and teach young children how to grow vegetables like Grandma Jan and Grandpa Jack taught me. And I want to grow trees for people to plant in places where there are no trees."

Michael's parents thought about this and said, "O.K., let's see what we can do to make this happen." They consulted his grandparents who were delighted with the idea. After much discussion with Michael, they all put together a plan.

Michael's Career and Return Home

And so Michael's career began. His mother's parents set aside a space on their land to begin Michael's nursery, and they helped him buy and propagate plants which he could sell. When spring arrived, they helped Michael with classes for the local primary school children so they could learn to grow vegetables. The school even set aside time and space for the children to have their own garden. They loved it!

Michael continued the school project and also successfully sold plants for nearly three years. Then he decided that it was time to 'green up' his neighbourhood. Michael had propagated lots of trees, and he had gotten permission from residents and the local authorities to plant these trees on people's properties and on public land. He invited children and their parents to help him with this special project, and many people from the community joined Michael in planting hundreds of trees. There were picnics on many tree-planting days, and the members of the community felt much closer to each other. They were also amazed at how much they had done and what an improvement the trees had made. Michael told everyone that these trees were the 'lungs of the earth' and that their environment was much better now that there were so many more trees.

Michael's projects had become so widespread that more money was needed to continue to fund all these activities. One day Grandpa Bill said to Michael, "We need more funds. Why don't we have piano concerts to raise money?" Michael played the piano beautifully, but he had never liked to play in front of people other than his family. Grandpa Bill assured him that he would also be a part of the concerts and that he and Michael could even play a few duets. And besides, they really did need money to continue with Michael's many projects. So Michael agreed, and they did two concerts a year—which were always sold out—at their town's Community Centre, and they raised money for the local school as well as for community greening projects. Sometimes other people in the community participated in the concerts as well, singing or playing other instruments.

During all this time Michael's sister, Claire, finished university and married a young man she had met there who shared her same passion for working with children with special needs. They moved to an area not far from her family, so Michael was able to see Claire quite often. He had missed her a lot when she was away for her studies. Claire had her first child—a little girl called Chloe—and Michael was amazed at how much like his sister she was. As soon as she could crawl, little Chloe followed Michael around just like Claire had done.

Meanwhile, Michael's nursery remained successful, and he continued his annual school projects and even took the 'greening' idea to other nearby neighbourhoods. People loved this young man and greatly admired his hard work and the beautiful results. Michael did all this valuable work for the community until his 27th year. One day, while at his beloved nursery, Michael collapsed. An ambulance came and took him to the hospital where it was discovered that Michael had a heart condition that no one had been aware of. The doctors made valiant attempts to save Michael's life, but nothing could be done. At his funeral, which was attended by the entire community, many people shared stories of how much young Michael had done to improve their local environment and to help their children appreciate plants and the Earth. Michael had been a kind and gentle person, and it had not mattered that he had been a little different from everyone else. He had seen things that they had not, and everyone cherished their experiences with this special young man.

At the time of Michael's death, Old Soul appeared with a smile and a hug. "Well, Michael," he said. "How was your first time on Earth?"

"It was amazing. I had so many interesting experiences. Some of them were really difficult but that was OK. I had the most wonderful parents, and grandparents who loved me very much, and a dear sister who was so patient with me. I couldn't have asked for a better family, and I'm truly happy that I went to Earth."

"Are you sad to be leaving Earth so soon?" asked Old Soul.

"Strangely, no," answered Michael. "I feel that I accomplished all I went there to do. I loved my family and I loved Mother Earth, and I was loved right back. I couldn't have asked for more."

"How do you feel about leaving your family behind?" Old Soul asked.

"Well, I can see how sad they are, and I want to do something about that. I'm still around them even though they can't see me, and I whisper to them in their thoughts, just like you used to do to me when I first arrived on Earth. At the moment they're all sleeping and, if you don't mind, I'm going to try to communicate with them."

"That's wonderful Michael! I'll see you later."

And so Michael visited his family in their dreams that night—his parents, grandparents, Claire and even little Chloe. They all smiled in their sleep and awoke with stories to share about Michael the next morning. Little Chloe had the most beautiful story of all because she had actually seen her Uncle Michael. "I sat on his lap and he kissed my cheek, and we talked for the longest time!" Chloe said excitedly. And, of course, everyone believed her because they felt that it was true.

Little Soul, who was no longer Michael, found himself heading back to familiar surroundings. Everything was so beautiful, and he remembered all the wonderful souls he had left behind when he decided to spend time on Earth. Everyone was there to celebrate his arrival and to welcome him back home. Little Soul visited with old friends and rested for a few days. Then a special group of souls asked him to meet with them. One member of the group said, "We're happy to hear that you enjoyed your time on Earth, Little Soul. Did you do everything that you wanted to do in your life?"

"I think so," Little Soul replied. "At times I was frustrated that a lot of people didn't understand me, but there was really nothing I could do about that. I was very lucky that I had such a special family to love and care for me. The love bit was really fantastic. It more than made up for the difficulties."

"Would you like to return to Earth?" Little Soul was asked. "You would start out as a baby once again, but not as Michael. Of course, you may choose your parents and decide what lessons you would like to learn during your lifetime. If you wish, a group of us can help with the planning of possibilities for some of your experiences. Think about it and let us know."

"OK," said Little Soul, and he went away to think.

"Do I really want to leave the Light of the Creator and return to Earth again now?" Little Soul asked himself. "Earth was pretty difficult at times." But then he remembered his loving Earth family, and he knew that he really did want to try again. He asked Old Soul if he could meet with the special planning group, and the meeting was arranged.

"What would you like to experience this time around?" the group wanted to know.

"Well, I would really like to be able to communicate normally this time, and I would like to grow up and have a life partner. My sister had a loving partner and a little girl and was so happy. I think I'd like to return as a girl this time around, and I'd like to help others with their Earth challenges."

"That's certainly possible, Little Soul, but you have only had one lifetime to experience the male energy. Are you sure you want to switch so soon? There will be plenty of other opportunities in the future."

"No, I think I'm ready," Little Soul replied. "Would it be possible for me to have a look at my parents now?"

"Yes," said a member of the group. "Look, here's one possibility."

Little Soul looked down and saw a young couple walking under a tree and holding hands in a lovely green park. They looked so peaceful and happy together. "Yes, I'll take them," Little Soul said.

"Are you certain?" he was asked. "We can show you some others if you'd like."

"No, I like these," Little Soul replied. And he then went off to meet with others to discuss a few possibilities for events in his next life. Some of the souls agreed to show up in Little Soul's new life at different times to provide him with clues about his life's purpose. One offered to be his best friend and another offered to be a potential life partner.

A short time later, Old Soul approached Little Soul and said, "Well, my friend, it's time for your journey to Earth again. I've come to see you off. Are you ready?"

"Yes, Old Soul," said Little Soul excitedly. "Thank you so much for all your help and friendship. Will you visit me on Earth this time?"

"Yes, in your early years, like before," Old Soul assured him. "And I'll always be available to you in your thoughts and dreams."

Celeste

Nine months of Earth time passed very quickly and the big day arrived! In a room with a young couple and a midwife, a beautiful baby left its womb world to begin a new life on Earth. "It's a little girl!" the midwife exclaimed. She then placed the baby into the arms of the mother who, along with the father, smiled and shed tears of joy. "Have you thought of a name for your daughter?" asked the midwife.

"Yes," her father answered. "She is Celeste."

"So I'm a little girl, and they're calling me Celeste. Wait until Old Soul hears this!"

"I'm right here," said Old Soul, "and Celeste is a fine name. I look forward to talking to you again soon. Right now, you need to have a little love exchange with your parents."

Celeste looked into the eyes of her mother and father for a long time and wished she could speak to them, but now she knew that this would have to wait. She enjoyed feeling the vibrations of their love for the longest time and then fell asleep.

Celeste was a happy baby who ate and slept well. She had two brothers—Sam who was 3 ½ and Tim who was 5—and they loved her dearly. They competed for the job of pushing Celeste in her little pram whenever they went for a walk, and they were both delighted the day came when Celeste was able to crawl and follow them around the house. And when Celeste took her first steps, the boys were ecstatic!

"Now we can put her in the sand pit!" exclaimed Sam.

"And we can pull her in our wagon," said Tim.

Their mother was a little less enthusiastic about their plans. "Celeste is still a baby," she said, "so we need to continue to watch over her carefully. I do not want her eating sand or falling out of a wagon."

Celeste continued to grow and thrive, and she survived all the worrisome plots and plans of her brothers, who continued to love her dearly. They even blew out her candles on her first and second birthday cakes but, when Celeste turned three, this stopped. She said in a defiant voice: "NO! I get to blow out the candles! It's MY cake!" And, with that, the boys' candle-blowing job was over, except for on their own birthdays, of course.

Celeste loved playing with Sam and Tim. She loved digging, climbing and playing with their trucks. Her parents kept giving her dolls for her birthdays and for Christmas, but Celeste didn't play with them very much. She preferred cars and trucks. "She's such a little tomboy! She spends too much time with her brothers," her parents' friends would say. But Celeste's parents were delighted that the children all got along so well. Disagreements were rare, and they played together for hours. The boys never minded when Celeste followed them around all the time, and they were very protective of her if any of their friends got too rough.

Celeste's Schooling

The first five years of Celeste's life passed quickly without any major catastrophes, and it was now time for her to begin kindergarten. Celeste was so happy because she had wanted to go to school with her brothers for a very long time. Now she could ride the school bus with them!

Celeste loved school and did very well. She got much better grades for her work than her brothers—not because she was smarter, but because she actually loved reading and learning about everything. She also loved playing with the other children on the school playground. The school had lots of equipment, and Celeste had a love of climbing. She would skip rope and swing with the other girls for a while, but climbing and other more active play always beckoned.

There was another girl in her class, Sally, who was also a tomboy, and the two of them became the best of friends. They visited each other's homes on weekends and could play and talk for hours. They created quite a stir at the school when, in Grade 6, they both wanted to try out for the boys' soccer team. "What should we do?" the adults pondered. "They are really good players but the team is only for boys." The girls argued that there was no girls' team so they should be allowed to play. And, with that, it was decided that they could play with the boys for that season. And guess what? The team won every game of the season for the first time ever. The school was awarded the regional trophy, and Celeste and Sally gained great respect from the boys (temporarily at least).

Celeste's time in primary school went very quickly. She seemed to soak up information like a sponge. Celeste wanted to know everything about EVERYTHING! Sometimes she asked questions even her teachers couldn't answer. "See if you can find that information on the Internet," they would say. Then THEY would go home and look on the Internet. Who says adults know everything?

When Celeste entered high school, her life really got exciting. She wanted to study so many things, and she loved having different teachers for different subjects. She also got excited about all the sports teams and was delighted to learn that the girls even had several teams of their own. Celeste signed up for the swimming team and the basketball team. The school counsellor thought she might approach things a little more realistically, but Celeste assured her that she had lots of energy and that she loved doing different things. She set records in school swimming competitions, and she was a star basketball player, along with her friend, Sally. The two girls had played basketball in the backyard with Celeste's brothers since their early childhood days, and they were fearless!

During the later years of high school, and then college, many of the boys and girls began dating, and some of them 'fell in love' as humans say. Celeste did not have a boyfriend and said that she was too busy to become involved in dating and things such as that, and she was. Not only did Celeste study very hard and participate in sports, but she was also introduced to the world of volunteering. Celeste had a neighbour, Rita, who ran a soup kitchen for the homeless, and she went with Rita one Sunday to help cook and serve lunch. It made Celeste very sad to see all the hungry people who lined up for the meal. She had not realised that there were so many people needing this kind of help and that they came in all ages—from children to the elderly. Celeste wanted to do more, so she helped Rita whenever she could.

Celeste finished college and was, in fact, number one in her class—the dux as Earth people say. Her parents and brothers were so proud. She received a small scholarship to help with university expenses, and she chose a school just a few hours' drive from her family. Once again, Celeste wanted to study everything, but she finally decided to try psychology and counselling. These subjects had not been offered to her in high school and college, and Celeste loved learning new things.

During her first weeks at university, Celeste confirmed something that she had often wondered about since childhood, but which she had always been too busy to ponder. In fact, she had to admit to herself that, in high school, she had at times deliberately kept herself too busy in order not to have to think about such things. Celeste did not want a boyfriend. She loved her brothers and had many boys who were her friends, but she was not attracted to them like other girls were. In fact, Celeste found herself more attracted to girls—one in particular.

Celeste met Paige on their first day at university. They soon discovered that they actually shared three classes, and they immediately became best friends. Outside of class, they sometimes talked together for hours and discovered that they had a lot of common interests. They had both decided that they wanted to go into some career where they could help others, but neither was sure exactly what that career would be. At the end of the first school year, they were dating regularly. Yes, at last, Celeste was 'in love.' And she was very happy about it. She hoped her parents would be able to share in her happiness.

The school year ended and both girls went home and got jobs for the summer in those places which sell 'fast food'. The money helped with their educational expenses, but the girls both learned that this would never be a career option for either of them. After a few weeks Paige came to visit Celeste on the weekend, and together they told Celeste's parents about their feelings for each other. To their surprise, it wasn't as much of a shock as they had feared. "I hope you aren't too disappointed," Celeste said. "I know you have always imagined a different life for me."

"Parents always imagine lives for their children," her mother replied. "While you're busy dreaming about being animal trainers, famous athletes and movie stars, we're busy imagining you as doctors, lawyers and college professors. Don't worry—children rarely ever become what their parents imagine. They have their own journey to make in life and their own dreams to pursue. And you have never been a disappointment to us. You have only brought us joy."

Celeste's parents hugged the girls and her father said, "What every parent really wants for their children is for them to be happy. That is the most important thing, and we can see that you are both very happy."

When the girls visited Paige's family, things went smoothly as well. Paige had already talked to her parents about her feelings regarding girls and boys during high school, so they welcomed Celeste, assuring her that they were happy that their daughter had found such a lovely partner. The girls then returned to their classes and continued with their schooling, enjoying their busy life on campus.

Love, Service, and the Return Home

Both Celeste and Paige completed counselling degrees and decided that they wanted to spend the rest of their lives together. "Do you think we should have a ceremony?" asked Celeste.

"I'd love to celebrate our relationship!" Paige replied. So the girls organised an event to recognise their union, and invited their families and friends. A ceremony was held outside on a beautiful day, and there were not many dry eyes, as everyone was truly happy to see two young people start a life together so much in love.

Celeste and Paige had a very long and happy life together. They both had known since they were teenagers that they wanted jobs where they actually helped people who were in need. Both of them had previously helped groups that fed the homeless, and they now wanted to do this in a serious way. They needed to earn money in order to feed themselves as well as the homeless, so Paige got a job as a counsellor in a drug rehabilitation centre, and Celeste got a job counselling young people who got into regular trouble with the police, often due to family breakdowns.

"Well, now that we can feed ourselves, perhaps we should start feeding and helping others," Celeste suggested. Paige agreed, so in the evenings and on weekends they began helping organisations feed homeless people in their area. They enjoyed talking to these people and hearing their stories. Some were teens who could no longer live at home due to problems with their parents which they couldn't figure out how to fix, some were middle-aged people who had lost long-time jobs and were now considered too old to hire, and there were those of all ages who were struggling with addictions of one kind or another and were unable to work. Celeste and Paige spent hours talking to these people and, on weekends, they often took someone home to have a shower. They bought lots of clothing at second-hand shops so were always prepared to offer a clean set of clothes.

Celeste and Paige loved being able to help so many people and couldn't imagine their lives being any other way. Sometimes they couldn't help everyone as much as they would have liked, and occasionally they lost someone through death. This saddened the girls, especially if it was a young person, but they accepted that everyone chooses his or her own path in life, and that at times people make choices with painful consequences. They were so grateful that they had both been raised in such loving and non-judgmental families.

After a few years the two young women had saved a deposit to put down on a modest house. They found a small 3-bedroom house on a street lined with beautiful trees and decided they wanted this to be their home. They were now able to help people in even more ways. At times there would be a family who had become homeless, and Celeste and Paige would take them home and look after them until a job and housing could be found.

Celeste and Paige never moved from their small home. After a number of years, they paid off the mortgage and had more spare money to continue helping people. This was their life's passion and they never considered it a burden. They often wished that they could help more. As they grew older, they became known around town as 'the two angels'. They looked after people until well into their nineties, and their compassion for those less fortunate was endless. As they aged, their activities became fewer, and they mostly cooked and fed homeless people and organised food and gifts for the poor at Christmas. At one point they decided to interview a number of homeless people and write their stories. These stories were compiled into a book that was sold to raise money for the homeless, as well as to raise community awareness of these people, and to show that they were human beings just like those who had homes.

Paige lived to be 99 and Celeste went on for another year after that. The town gave her a big party for her 100th birthday, and she died peacefully in her sleep that very night. At her funeral her friends were saying how strange it was that Celeste had died right after her 100th birthday party. Then someone said, "Actually this was very typical of Celeste. She always crammed as many activities as possible into one day!" Everyone had a chuckle and then shared their memories of this special person who had given so much to the community.

Brief Welcome Home
and a New Life

Upon Celeste's death, the souls of all her old friends were there to greet her as she returned to her home in the Light of the Creator. Included in the group were those who had been her parents, her brothers, her partner Paige, her childhood friend Sally, and hundreds of those whom she had helped during her lifetime. And, of course, Old Soul was there. They intermingled all of their energies into one big hug and had a wonderful celebration.

After the party was over, Old Soul asked Celeste, "How did you enjoy that very long life?"

"It was wonderful!" Celeste replied. "I had such a fantastic family and a beautiful loving partner, and I met so many special people. It was a rich and full life. I couldn't have asked for more."

"Would you like to return to Earth?" asked Old Soul.

"Why, yes!" Celeste exclaimed. "But this time I think I would like a life that is not quite as busy as the last two. You know, one that is what humans call 'normal'."

Old Soul chuckled. "My Friend, don't you realise what 'normal' actually is? It's just another human label!"

Both souls laughed heartily. Then Little Soul, who was no longer Celeste, went off to talk to other souls about possibilities for a new life.

A few days later Old Soul came to see Little Soul again. "Well, Little Soul, are you ready to visit Earth once more?" he asked.

"Of course!" said Little Soul. "I can't wait to get back!"

Old Soul then asked, "What would you like to experience this time around? Are there new things you'd like to do?"

"I think I'd be happy with a very short life this time," answered Little Soul. "There are a couple of my old friends who have returned as parents for a particular lesson which will increase compassion for many people, and I'd like to help them. They are already living on Earth and are preparing for their first child. I'd really love to be that baby."

"Well, let's have a look, Little Soul. I can see Miriam and Mitchell. Are they the ones?"

"Yes, they are. This lifetime won't require as much planning, so I'd like to join them right away if I may."

"Well, Little Soul, it has been a short reunion, and I'll miss you around Home, but this is a perfect time for you to travel to Earth once again so, if you're certain, I'll say 'goodbye' for now."

"Thanks, Old Soul. We'll catch up again when I get back. I should have a few more interesting adventures and lessons to share with you." Then Little Soul shouted "Goodbye!" as he headed for Earth.

A Short Life

Miriam and Mitchell were in the delivery room at the hospital. They had waited nine months for this exciting day and were so happy to be having their first baby. Miriam had been in labour for nearly a day and was very tired. Little Soul was also very tired. He'd been in that narrow birth canal for a very long time and really wanted his freedom.

"O.K., Miriam, give us one more big push," said the midwife.

Miriam pushed very hard and out popped a baby boy. He was too tired to even breathe, but after the midwife worked on him for a bit, Little Soul made a coughing sound followed by a little cry. Then he was cleaned up and handed to his mother, who wept with joy. His father also shed a few happy tears of relief.

"Do you have a name for your baby?" asked the midwife.

"Yes, we will call him Nathan," his father replied.

Old Soul suddenly appeared to Little Soul, who was of course the only one who could see him, and said "Well, Little Soul, we meet again! What a journey you have had coming into this world. Rest a bit while you adjust to being Nathan, and we'll talk later."

Nathan slept while the midwife and a doctor examined him. His mother was taken to another room where she also slept after such a long labour and birth. Even his father fell asleep in a chair, after having had no sleep for nearly two days.

A few hours later a doctor came into the room where Nathan's parents had been sleeping. "In a few minutes your son will be brought to you. Before he arrives, I must tell you that there is a problem. It appears that his heart has not formed properly, and there is nothing we can do to correct it. You may take him home if you wish, but we can't tell you how long he will live. It could be a few days, a few weeks or, at best, a few months. I'm very sorry."

Nathan's parents felt numb with the shock of the news. Before they had a chance to talk to each other, a nurse brought Nathan to them. His mother held him tightly while his father stroked his tiny head. When his little eyes opened and looked at them, they both said, "We love you so much." And then they lovingly took turns holding their tiny son for a very long time.

As soon as little Nathan fell asleep again, Old Soul appeared. "Well, Nathan," he said, "as you know, all earthly lifetimes are different, but it looks like this one is truly going to be a new experience. I may be seeing you back Home much earlier this time around."

"Well, I wasn't expecting a long life journey this time, but it looks like it might be really, really short. It will be interesting to see how things play out. It appears that the decisions to be made in this lifetime will be made by my parents. I wonder how my leaving early will affect them."

"Before you left the Light of the Creator, Nathan, you did say that this life was to assist Miriam and Mitchell in raising compassion here on Earth. It looks like your chance to do this will be coming quite soon. I will be there to see you when you make your transition and, of course, I'm always available if you need me."

After three days, Nathan went home with his parents. He drank a bit of his mother's milk from time to time, but mostly he slept. Whenever he was awake, his parents always lovingly held him, smiled, and talked softly to him. Nathan felt nothing but pure love, and it was wonderful.

On the 45th day of his life, Nathan was suddenly overwhelmed by a totally peaceful feeling as he lay in his mother's arms. He decided not to open his eyes, and his thoughts were focused on the Creator's Light. Old Soul appeared and said, "Well, Nathan, it looks like you are contemplating your return Home. Let me know when you are ready."

Little Nathan smiled in his sleep, and then his tiny body suddenly went limp. "Let's go, Old Soul. My work here is done." And off they went to join old friends in their heavenly Home.

Nathan's mother was aware of the exact moment when Nathan left his little body. She called to his father, and they both kissed Nathan's little face and wept.

Upon his return Home, Nathan continued to observe his parents from the Light of the Creator. He watched them as they tearfully buried his little body and mourned his absence. He watched his mother as she spent time in his room, holding his soft toys and sniffing his scent left on his little blankets. He watched Miriam and Mitchell grieve for several months until, suddenly one day, they decided that they wanted to honour Nathan's life by helping other people. They sat down at their computer, went online, and set up a support group for parents who had lost babies. They put some precious little photos they had taken of Nathan onto their website, told the story of his short life, and invited other grieving parents to do the same. They arranged meetings in person with grieving parents in their area, inviting others to also do this. They set up a group to visit parents in hospital, when their babies had died shortly before or after birth. They personally helped anyone they could, and they encouraged others to do the same. At times they even collected and donated money to help parents with funeral expenses. They wanted everyone to be able to celebrate the life of any precious child they had lost.

Nathan was amazed at all the wonderful things his parents had done. He said to Old Soul, "Now I truly understand how Miriam and Mitchell increased compassion on Earth, and I can actually see the vibration of that planet raising. I'm so happy that I got to be their son."

"Well, Nathan, now that you're Little Soul again, do you think you'd like to make another trip to Earth?" asked Old Soul.

"Definitely," answered Little Soul. "And do you know what, Old Soul? I want another life as another child of Miriam and Mitchell—a longer one this time!"

"Why not!" said Old Soul. "It is your choice after all."

A New Challenge

Little Soul continued to return to Earth many times, having new experiences and learning new lessons. Each time he returned Home, Little Soul was amazed at how easily he could forget about the Light of the Creator while living on Earth. He was also amazed at how unaware he was that, each time he entered Earth, he brought with him the memory of things he had previously experienced. He couldn't believe that he remained so unaware of plans he made while in the Light of the Creator, and of others agreeing to be with him to help during his Earthly life. He also couldn't believe how easy it was to forget that choices were always his—at Home as well as on Earth.

"Old Soul," said Little Soul after one of his many returns Home, "I think I'm ready for a truly difficult life. I've already had lots of challenges, and I know that I have helped to raise the Earth's vibration, but I feel that the level of compassion there really needs to lift dramatically for life to continue in a peaceful and meaningful way. I've given it lots of thought and I think I'm ready to be a refugee."

"Well," said Old Soul, "that truly is a great challenge. And it is an amazing way to create the compassion needed for the positive evolvement of life on Earth. And there have never been more opportunities for a person to have this experience. If you are certain that this is what you want to do, then you should have a planning session with other souls so you can have some of the experiences you feel you need. You have come such a long way, Little Soul!"

Little Soul met with other souls who agreed to be those whom he would need—family, friends, teachers, and even some who would appear briefly with words or insights that would help Little Soul remember his purpose. Then he went to Old Soul and said, "I have chosen my parents and am now ready for my next Earthly experience. I'll see you when I get back!"

Little Soul entered Earth and was born at a small hospital in a land where he had never been before. This time Little Soul was a girl, and her parents were Soraya and Reza. She was their first child and they named her Samira. When Samira was handed to her mother, Soraya whispered to her, "You are a special little girl and you will do wonderful things."

At this point little Samira fell asleep, and Old Soul came for their first visit and chat. "Well, Little Soul, this time around you are Samira, and I must say you are truly a beautiful baby. As always, I will come to visit you occasionally during the first few years of life here. If you need my help, just let me know and I'll be there. And remember that you're never alone, no matter what happens, and you are always loved."

The first two years of Samira's life were happy and peaceful. She was surrounded by family who loved her and had lots of cousins around to play with. Samira walked very early—at only nine months—and could point at many things and say the names of the items when she was just a year old.

Her mother would often whisper to her as Samira was falling asleep, "Remember that you are my special little girl, and I know some day you will do wonderful things."

Samira loved her parents and followed them everywhere. When Reza would return from work at the end of the day, she would run to him and he would pick her up and do a little dance. "How's Daddy's beautiful little girl?" he would ask. Then he would sit down and cuddle Samira and sing to her while dinner was being prepared. Samira loved those quiet moments as much as the time spent running around and playing chasing games.

When Samira celebrated her second birthday her home was filled with family. Both sets of grandparents were there, along with three sets of aunts and uncles and eight cousins. Everybody brought food, each family had their specialty, and all of it was delicious. The kids quickly ate their lunch so they could have their favourite part of the meal which, of course, was lots of yummy dessert. Then they ran outside to play, leaving the grown-ups to talk in peace.

Reza seemed a bit concerned as he began to talk to the family. "At work yesterday some people mentioned that there is fighting going on in a village not far from here. They are worried that it might spread. One has family who have left that area and have come here to stay for a while until it looks safe enough to go back. Hopefully things will work out soon and peace will be restored. I'll keep you informed of any other events I hear about. For now, let's return to more happy topics so the kids won't get upset."

A few weeks passed and everything seemed normal, but there were a few rumours from visitors who reported that there was indeed fighting not too far away, and that it seemed to be spreading to other areas. People were beginning to flee their homes in search of safety. They had hoped the fighting would stop, but people's homes were being broken into in the middle of the night with demands made for food, accommodation, money, and men to help them fight.

Suddenly Reza and Soraya found themselves in this very situation when a group of men with guns burst into their home whilst everyone was asleep. "Cook us some food!" they demanded of Soraya, who was terrified.

After the men were fed, they said "We're not here to hurt you. We just need money, weapons, supplies, and men to help us fight government officials. We're here to bring changes that will make our country better. Give us your car keys. We need your car tonight. And give us any money you have and your mobile phone. We need to make some important calls. Tomorrow morning, we will bring your car and phone back and collect the other things we need. We will be encouraging all strong men to join our army. For now, get some sleep. We'll talk more tomorrow. When you hear what we have to say, I'm sure you will want to help."

Soraya and Reza had no intention of sleeping. They quickly gathered little Samira along with her stroller, some clothes, food, bank documents, Passports, and jewellery which could be sold for money if necessary. Then they sneaked away from the village and headed towards a rural area where there had been no fighting.

"I wish we could have warned others in the village," said Soraya.

"We couldn't," replied Reza. "There were lights in other houses, so there must have been others whose homes were invaded like ours. There was no time to sneak to other homes, and it was too risky. Our neighbours will have to make their own decisions about what they want to do. Meanwhile, if we keep walking, we will reach my Cousin Ahmed's village in a few hours, and we'll discuss the situation with his family to see what plans we can come up with."

Soraya, Reza and little Samira reached Ahmed's house at dawn. Ahmed had just awakened and was both surprised and alarmed at their arrival. "Cousin, this does not look like a social visit," he said. "Come in and tell me everything while I make a pot of tea."

Reza told Ahmed all about the invasion of his home, while Soraya fed breakfast to little Samira in another room. "Well," said Ahmed, "I hope they don't come here, but I definitely need to make some plans just in case. Mother and Father are getting old, and Father has really slowed down in recent years. For now, what would you like to do? You are welcome to stay here as long as you'd like."

"Thank you, Cousin, but I really feel that we should get out of here as soon as possible. We would like to rest today, as we got very little sleep last night, and we are exhausted from the long walk here. We'll stay one night and leave early tomorrow morning. Meanwhile, could I make a call on your mobile phone? My mother and father are still living with my eldest brother, and I need to find out if the rebels have invaded their end of town."

Ahmed handed his phone to Reza who dialled his brother's number. "No one is answering," he said. "I don't know if that's good or bad. We'll have to wait and see."

"I need a few things from the markets so I'll drive you there tomorrow," suggested Ahmed. "Meanwhile, my parents will be getting up soon, so let's just pretend that someone has dropped you off for a short visit to catch up with family. I'll wait until the right time to tell them what has actually happened. I don't wish to worry them until absolutely necessary."

And so Reza, Soraya and little Samira had their visit and chatted as if everything in life was normal. The next morning, they said 'goodbye' to Reza's aunt and uncle, and Ahmed drove them to the markets in a nearby town. They thanked Ahmed and hugged him, holding back their tears. "I'll pray for you," Ahmed said, and they parted, wondering if they would ever see each other again.

Reza and Soraya decided to stay in the little town until late in the day, when the temperature would be cooler and easier for walking. They relaxed, talked casually to a few people to see what news had reached that area, withdrew what money they could from the local bank, purchased a good meal, and pretended to be tourists. At sunset the couple set off with Samira in her stroller, preparing to walk as far as they could in the coolness of the night. They were heading for a larger town where they could catch a bus to other places. They knew they would need to walk in darkness and rest during the hot part of the day, and that it would take two days to reach the town. Along the way, they ate stale bread they had brought from home and some fruit they had bought at the market. They also had a few bottles of water.

Soraya and Reza arrived at the town just before dawn. They were exhausted and were grateful that Samira was quietly sleeping in her stroller. They waited until daylight and checked into accommodation for the day. They washed themselves, and Soraya rinsed their clothes and hung them out to dry on a little balcony. Then they had a meal, after which

Reza took Samira for a stroll while Soraya slept. When Samira became tired, Reza returned to the room, and everyone slept soundly for a few hours.

When the family awoke, they went to the bank where Reza and Soraya were able to withdraw most of the remaining money from their account. They checked the bus schedules, selected a town they wished to travel to, bought their tickets, and went shopping for a few simple food items and bottles of water for the trip. When they boarded the bus, it felt so good not having to walk for another day. Their legs and backs were still aching.

It took nearly nine hours for the family to reach their destination. The bus travelled through the night, which enabled them to get some sleep. Little Samira slept soundly and her parents were grateful. When they got off the bus, they immediately checked into accommodation for two days to give them time to plan what to do next. They had a good meal, and Reza purchased a new mobile phone. He tried to ring his brother again but still there was no answer. He could only hope that his family members were safe. He rang Ahmed to thank him for his hospitality, and Ahmed told him that he had also tried unsuccessfully to ring Reza's brother. Also, Ahmed had not received any news of how things were going in Reza's town.

The couple pushed Samira around in her stroller for much of the day, pretending to be tourists. They chatted with people here and there, but never told anyone about their true situation, as they did not know whom they could trust. In the evening Reza spent time in the sitting room at their accommodation watching television, while Soraya gave Samira a bath and played with her until her little eyes began to droop with sleepiness. Soraya thought about how sweet her little daughter was. She rarely complained or cried, and actually smiled much of the time. The only complaint she had made during this ordeal was to say, "I'm hungry," and that was understandable since she truly was. Soraya felt sad that her little girl was having to live in such difficult times. It was not the life she had hoped for.

Reza returned and reported what he had seen on the TV news. "Our town is under attack. The rebels returned and some of the men joined them. Others resisted, and some have been beaten and taken prisoner. A few have even been killed. Part of the town has been set on fire. I don't know what has happened to our family and friends. We can only pray for them and hope they escaped."

"Did you tell anyone that we were from that town?" asked Soraya.

"No, I was afraid there might be rebel sympathisers here," replied Reza. "Tomorrow, we need to make arrangements to leave and cross the border into a neighbouring country to make sure we are safe for now."

That night the couple slept, but not very peacefully as they were so worried. They were grateful that at least little Samira slept soundly. At dawn they awoke to the beautiful sound of a bird singing on their balcony. Reza and Soraya listened to the bird for a while as they watched the sun rise, not knowing when another such beautiful moment might arrive in their lives.

When Samira awoke, her parents took her downstairs where they had breakfast, and then pushed her in her stroller to the business district. They purchased bus tickets to travel the next morning to a small town which bordered a neighbouring country. Their idea was to seek permission to enter that country as tourists who would be visiting relatives. Reza did have a cousin living there, but wasn't sure if he had moved to another address. He hoped he wouldn't have to be too specific with the location.

The family spent the rest of the day walking around town and enjoying a little park where Samira could run around and play. Late in the afternoon they had a meal at a local market and purchased some food and water for their trip. They returned to their accommodation house to pack and hopefully get a good night's rest for their ten-hour bus trip the next day.

Samira was really tired after her long day so Soraya gave her a bath and put her to bed. Then, while she packed up all their belongings, Reza went to see what news might be on the TV. The news that he returned with was not good.

"You're not going to believe this, but the rebels have now entered the town that we just left. Things do not look good. I tried to ring my brother again but still there was no answer. Then I tried to ring Ahmed but again got no answer. The sooner we get out of this place, the better!"

The only member of the family who slept peacefully that night was Samira. Her parents went to bed early but tossed and turned all night, worrying about their trip the next day and their future. They had never imagined that life could be like this, and they prayed for the strength to get through any difficulties they might face.

The bus trip was long but not entirely unpleasant. There was another young couple with a little girl Samira's age, and the two girls shared fruit, pointed to things they could see out the window, and talked and giggled much of the time. The parents introduced themselves and talked a little bit, but were quite careful about what they discussed. Soraya felt that this couple, too, were in a similar situation but couldn't say anything because one never knew who might be listening.

When the bus finally stopped and everyone got off, Reza discovered that they were within walking distance of the border of the country they wanted to enter. It was too late to ask permission for entry so he got accommodation nearby. The room was tiny and they had to share a bathroom with others, but at least it was only for one night.

The next morning Reza and Soraya pushed Samira in the stroller to the border and presented their Passports at the gate. When they were asked their reason for entry, Reza gave them the name of his cousin and the address that he had, and said they wanted to visit for one month. The border patrol said that they would grant them entry for two weeks, after which time they would need to re-apply. The couple happily agreed, paid the money they were asked for, crossed the border and walked a short distance. When they were out of sight of everyone, Reza got out his mobile phone and dialled the number he had for his cousin. It had been disconnected so, once again, the couple had to find accommodation and try to find out any news they could while making further plans. How they missed their home and family! Everything now seemed like a distant dream.

While the family slept that night, Old Soul had a visit with little Samira. It had been quite a while since their last chat.

"Well, how's life as a refugee?" Old Soul asked. "Is it anything like you imagined?"

"Not at all," responded Samira. "I never could have imagined how hard this journey would be for my parents. I feel so sorry for them. They are such lovely people and I am too little to help them. It is really challenging having to travel from place to place all the time, and I know they are living in fear for the future."

"Well, Samira, I guess you remember that time is different in the Light of the Creator. There is no past, present and future but everything exists all at once, so I can tell you that your little family will get a bit of a rest very soon. It won't last forever—nothing ever does—but it will restore everyone's strength for a while. We'll talk again when things get difficult. Meanwhile, have a peaceful night's sleep." And, with that, Old Soul left Samira with pleasant dreams.

And Old Soul was right! The very next day Reza left Soraya and Samira sleeping while he went to a local market to buy some fruit and bread. He noticed a carpenter's stall displaying tables, chairs, and cabinets with drawers and doors. This was the kind of work that Reza had done in his hometown, and it seemed so long ago. He stopped to talk to the carpenter, whose name was Nadim, and they got on straight away. Nadim offered Reza a job building cabinets for a large new house being built in a nearby town. Reza explained that he was on a visitor's visa, and that he had a wife and daughter who would need a place to live. Nadim assured Reza that he would not inform the authorities of his whereabouts, and he told him that his family would be welcome to stay in a room at the back of his building shed. This room had been built to house other workers in past years, and the shed also had a small toilet and sink. The family could use the shower and kitchen in his house.

Little Samira and her parents lived comfortably with these arrangements for nearly a year. They got on well with Nadim and his wife, Sara, and Reza enjoyed the work. They were still unable to contact family back home, and the news on TV continued to be worrisome. Just as the family began to feel settled, a friend of Nadim approached him at the markets where he and Reza were shopping for lumber. He reported that there had been recent incidents with refugees in a nearby town, and that action was soon to be taken to remove all refugees from the area.

Soraya's heart sank as Reza and Nadim shared the news upon their return. "What will we do?" she asked.

"I'm sorry, but we have to leave," Reza replied. "Nadim and Sara, thank you from the bottom of our hearts for this wonderful period of peace and friendship. We'll never forget your kindness. We will leave this place tonight."

"It has been an honour to know your family and to work with you," Nadim replied. "Here is the remaining money I owe you for all your hard work." Nadim opened his wallet and gave Reza a generous wad of money.

Tears filled his eyes as Reza accepted the money and hugged Nadim, while Soraya and Sara also hugged. "You have no idea what this means to us," Reza said.

"My brother, I will drive you to town where you can catch a bus tonight. May God bless and watch over your family."

That night, while she and her parents were on the bus, Samira slept and Old Soul visited. "Well, Samira, I see you are a traveller once more. How are you feeling?"

"Well, Old Soul, I was really happy living with Nadim and Sara. Now we're homeless again and my parents are so worried. I wish I could help them, but I can't. Being a refugee is even harder than I had imagined when I planned this life before coming to Earth."

"Well, Samira, I will tell you that things are going to get even more difficult. In order to increase compassion on Earth, it's going to take a lot of suffering from a lot of people like your family. But, don't worry—eventually there will be many people who see the suffering and want it stopped, and they will demand that the Earth's leaders come together to deal with the refugees in a compassionate manner. It will be necessary for all countries to consult and come up with a plan together before the situation can truly be made better. And you, little Samira, will have a role in all this. But, enough talk—it's time for you to wake up and give your parents one of those beautiful smiles to warm their hearts."

The Journey Continues

Samira and her parents spent the next four years moving from place to place on foot. Often they travelled with others who were also escaping the violence that had taken over their towns. They all just wanted a peaceful life and a future for their children. Occasionally they had to sneak across borders to other countries, and sometimes they were caught and forced to return to areas outside towns they were trying to reach. Sometimes one of the group would successfully sneak into a town and buy food at a local market. This food was then shared with others. Many times, there was no food, so everyone went hungry.

Little Samira never complained, no matter how difficult things became. She always had a smile for everyone and went around hugging those who looked sad. Sometimes she would put her little lips to someone's ear and whisper, "I love you." Samira was known as the 'Little Comforter' by others in the group. Whenever they had a long journey on foot, she would hold the hands of other little children who were exhausted from so much walking, and she would sing to them to cheer them up. Reza and Soraya felt blessed to have such a special little girl.

One day someone came back with food and news that there were people who were loading boats with refugees and taking them to a distant country across the water, where they could settle down and start a new life. Everyone became quite excited with this news. Reza and Soraya felt immediately that this was the opportunity they had been waiting for, and it had come just in time, as all their money was gone and they were having to sell Soraya's jewellery to be able to have food to eat. They met with the man who was organising the boats, and he agreed to let them make the journey in exchange for what remained of Soraya's jewellery, some pieces of which were precious family heirlooms and very valuable. Reza felt sad that his wife had to give up everything she possessed but Soraya said, "These are just 'things' and are not important. Life is very precious and we need to preserve it for Samira."

Early the next morning the passengers gathered while it was still dark. When they saw the boat, many were shocked, as it didn't look very safe or seaworthy. As they were desperate, and most had no money left, everyone climbed aboard to begin their journey.

After three days the passengers began to feel really scared. First, there was almost no food or water left, and then the wind had picked up, making the sea very rough. Suddenly a giant wave washed over the boat and it capsized. Samira was ripped from her father's arms by another huge wave, and then Old Soul appeared. "So, we meet again, Samira. How are you feeling?"

"I feel quite free," answered Samira. "I'm actually looking down at myself and my parents, who are so frightened. I wish I could comfort them."

"That opportunity will come later," replied Old Soul. "You will soon see what a difference your short little life has made. For now, come along with me as you continue your transition. As you know, time is not linear in the Creator's Light so I can actually show you a bit of the future if you'd like."

"I'd love that!" exclaimed Samira.

As she looked down at Earth, Samira saw her father wandering along the shoreline and looking very distraught. Suddenly he saw something on the beach in the distance and hurried to get a better look. It was Samira, and Reza let out a loud wail as he scooped up the lifeless body of his precious little girl.

Next, Samira observed television cameras filming the refugees who had survived and were gathered together on the beach—some crying, and others looking numb from shock. All of a sudden, she saw her mother run to her father, who was approaching with her little body. Her parents wept as they hugged their most precious possession.

Then Samira was shown people being interviewed. These were refugees who had spent time with Samira's family in various travels and camps. They had seen a photo of Samira on the TV news and immediately recognised her. "She was our Little Comforter," one of them said. "If we began feeling despair, she seemed to know and would come and give us a hug and sit on our laps. She was an Angel on Earth and now has returned to be an Angel with the Creator."

And then Samira was shown a most amazing thing. There was a special centre for assisting refugees, and one section had a beautiful garden inside where people could sit amongst trees and ferns in a peaceful setting. And this section had a name—Samira's Place! There was even a plaque with Samira's life story as a refugee. Samira looked at Old Soul in amazement.

"See," said Old Soul, "one life can make a difference. Your story has gone global and compassion for refugees is increasing on Earth. Gradually more people are realising that they can make a difference, and they are forming groups and taking action."

"Thank you for that future glimpse, Old Soul. Now I must go back and visit my parents."

Samira's spirit returned to Earth briefly to console Soraya and Reza. As it happened, this return was actually at little Samira's funeral, where a dove suddenly appeared and sat on her mother's shoulder, while Samira gave her parents a hug of energy and whispered in their ears, "I love you." Her parents looked at each other at the same moment in amazement, and then wept as Samira's little coffin was lowered into the ground.

An Evolving Earth

Little Soul was greeted once more by Old Soul and other Souls who had gathered to welcome him home. "Wow, Little Soul! What a life! What will you do now? Will you return to Earth again?" they asked excitedly.

"Definitely!" replied Little Soul. "I have learned so much and I already know what kind of changes I would like to see on Earth now. The seeds for these changes have already been planted, and I realise that they may take years to develop, but I feel ready for the necessary challenges. The long-term future I see for Earth is so bright. I can't wait to get back!"

Later, when Little Soul met with the planning group to discuss plans for his next Earthly life, he was asked, "What changes on Earth are you thinking about participating in, Little Soul?"

"Well, I have noticed what I can only describe as a battle between the Light and the Dark, or the new energy striving to replace the old energy. The old energy is afraid of change and is trying to maintain its control over Earthly events. It is trying to get rid of the new energy which is optimistically working on creating an Earth which is evolving into a planet of higher consciousness which will benefit the entire Universe. I would like to return as a part of the Light to help lift the Earth."

"That sounds amazing, Little Soul," responded a member of the planning group. "We'll let you get on with your plans. Please call on us if you require any assistance." Then the planning group left Little Soul to ponder his next life.

Little Soul met with Old Soul to discuss a few ideas. "Old Soul, I have realised how tired I am of wars being fought on Earth, and I would like to participate in the beginning of the ending of these wars. I don't know how I might accomplish this, but my intent is so strong that I am sure I will be able to make a positive difference."

"That's wonderful, Little Soul. I'm sure you will definitely make positive changes on Earth. I'll leave you to have a chat with those who will be there to help you in some way in your next life." And Old Soul disappeared to give Little Soul the opportunity to work out some plans for that next life.

Little Soul discussed a few possibilities with several other Souls, and after arrangements had been made for one to be his best friend on Earth, and another to be there to remind him of his intent, Little Soul announced that he was ready to enter Earth once more, and that he had even chosen his parents. And after saying "Goodbye" to the other Souls, Little Soul left for his next Earthly adventure.

When Little Soul entered Earth this time, he was beginning life in yet another country where he had never lived in any other life. He was the first child born to Daniela and Vadim, and his birth went smoothly. The midwife cleaned his little body and handed him to Daniela, who held him close to her heart. Then the midwife asked his parents, "Have you chosen a name for your son?"

"Yes," replied Vadim. "We will call him Symon." Then Vadim asked to hold his son, and he and Daniela smiled and shed tears of joy as tiny Symon looked into their eyes, seeming to smile back at them.

Soon the baby fell asleep, and immediately Old Soul appeared. "Well, Little Soul, you are now Symon, and your parents seem very happy to have you in their lives. As always, I will visit you from time to time during your early years, and you are always free to call on me in your thoughts if you feel you need any assistance. For now, I will leave you to enjoy a peaceful sleep."

Life as a Soldier

Little Symon's first few years of life went quite smoothly. Vadim was in the army, where he maintained and repaired all kinds of equipment, and Daniela was a nurse. They were very loving parents who gave Symon lots of freedom to play with other children and to explore and learn. When he reached five years of age and began attending kindergarten, Symon was so happy. He knew a lot of the children, as they lived near him, but he also met some new ones, one of whom was Anton, who was destined to become his best friend.

Symon and Anton remained friends for all of their school years. Neither of them had any siblings, so they actually felt like brothers. They could talk to each other about anything—school problems, girlfriend problems, home problems—and there was no judgment and no fear that their conversations would be shared with anyone else. It was a relationship of trust that others often envied, and it continued all the way through high school.

After the boys graduated from high school, their fathers, who were both in the army, wanted them to undergo at least a year of military training to prepare them for any future problems in their country. Their area was peaceful, but there were other areas not too far away that sometimes had a few skirmishes with a nearby aggressive country whose army often entered other countries in an attempt to take part of a country and make it their own. Usually this was done when an area had resources that would benefit the aggressive country.

Symon and Anton agreed to undergo the training and, after the year had passed, Anton decided that he wanted to go to university to study medical science, as he had always wanted to do research. He and Symon had dinner together the evening before he left to attend a university in a neighbouring country. "Well, Anton," Symon said, "I am going to miss you, but I am happy that you have decided what you want to do in life, and I know that you will make a positive difference on this Earth." Then they hugged, wished each other all the best, and vowed to stay in touch.

Symon remained with his parents and continued his military training, as he hadn't been able to figure out exactly what it was that he wanted to do with his life. He didn't really want to fight in a war, but he did want to be able to help out in the event that something like this happened. He also learned a lot of useful life skills, such as First Aid and caring for those who had been injured in battle. His mother suggested to Symon that he might want to consider becoming a nurse like herself, but Symon didn't think so. He just couldn't seem to figure out exactly what it was that he truly wanted to do.

After another year had passed, troublesome events began to occur in an area of a nearby country. This area was beautiful and had many resources. It had a reliable and clean water supply and lots of fertile land, which provided crops for the entire country as well as for several nearby countries. It was also the home of the university which Anton was attending, and this really worried Symon.

Soon the aggressive country became impatient with the country they had invaded, because that country refused to give up the area which the invading country wanted. The invading soldiers then began bombing the area, destroying homes and businesses and even taking lives. They thought this would make the invaded country surrender that area of land, as this was what had always happened in the past when an area had been attacked, but not this time. The invaded country had a new leader, and his thinking was very different from the leaders of the past. He said that they would not surrender and that, if necessary, they would fight to keep all of their country.

The leader put out a request for assistance, and soldiers came from all areas of his country, as well as from bordering countries. Even Symon came to help defend the area under attack, and he was reunited with Anton who had joined the soldiers who were striving to keep their country intact. Anton also was not keen to go into battle, so he and Symon decided to stay in places that were near areas of attack by the aggressor. They helped residents who were not fighting to move into places that would offer them some protection, such as basements. They also helped those who wished to take their children and leave the area to evacuate to another town, or even a nearby country, until the fighting was over.

"It's so wonderful to see the courage of this country's new leader in his refusal to surrender any part of the country. Do you think his soldiers will go to the invading country to retaliate soon?" Symon asked Anton.

"No," replied Anton. "This leader has a totally different view of things. He is not driven by fear, and he does not seek revenge. He only wants to protect his country and to keep it intact into the future for its citizens. He will fight to defend this country and will ask for assistance from other countries for any additional weapons, supplies and soldiers he needs to do this. Some have already sent weapons, and it will be interesting to see how other countries respond. This man gives me a feeling of hope for the future, even though things seem pretty grim at the moment."

"Well," responded Symon, "I certainly hope other countries will offer support. This country is so much smaller than the attacker's country, and help is definitely needed."

The battle continued month after month and many countries sent needed supplies, including weapons, tanks and missiles. Even more soldiers from other countries volunteered to join the battle. People in other parts of the world couldn't believe how such a small defending country could prevent such a large aggressive country from taking their land. Other countries helped with food and medicine, and even accepted people who had fled the country under attack, when their homes had been completely destroyed and they needed to take their children to an area that was safe. It was the first time that anyone had experienced such a positive response to such destructive aggression, and things seemed different on Earth. The aggressor was condemned worldwide, and there was actually hope that people in his own country would eventually stop him, as it was obvious that he had attacked the other country for no other reason than the desire for more power. As many of his soldiers died in battle, the aggressor forced other young men without training into the army, and the parents of these young men were very angry with their leader. People in other parts of the world began to feel that the aggressor would not be tolerated as a leader by his country much longer.

Symon and Anton moved from community to community to help as each area was attacked. One day they had an unexpected surprise when they were summoned to a building in the area they were preparing to defend, and discovered that the country's leader was in this building, meeting with all the soldiers and thanking them for their hard work and dedication. Symon was overcome with a strong feeling that he was somehow connected to this leader, but he didn't know how. It was a strange feeling that in some way they had shared something in the past. The leader came over to Symon and personally thanked him for leaving his own country to help, and he told Symon that he had an unusually strong feeling that Symon was very courageous and that he would soon participate in something that would significantly change things. "I'll do my very best to defend your country," Symon replied. "And I thank you for your leadership in not letting the aggressor steal any areas. I feel that this is making a positive change, not just for your country, but for the whole world."

"Thank you," said the leader. "And thank you for risking your life to also help with positive change. Not everyone understands this. You are a special young man."

Very early the next morning, Symon decided to join a group of soldiers who were going to sneak up on the aggressor's army and blow up their tanks, to prevent them from entering the area they were planning to take over. He and Anton hugged as the group prepared to leave on this mission. "Well, my brother," Anton said, "this is something different for you, and I must admit that I am worried. I will hold you in my thoughts."

The group found a secluded area where they could make their plans. They needed to create some sort of distraction so the invading troops would not suspect what was about to happen. Symon offered to move to another spot and start shooting to draw the invaders' attention away from the real threat. The others were concerned about his safety as he did not usually do things like this, but they agreed to the plan as it seemed to be very good for the situation they were facing.

Symon secretly positioned himself behind a canopy of large trees and suddenly began to fire rounds of ammunition close to some men who were eating breakfast around a fire near the tanks. The surprised men began to fire back, and some of them ran to the tanks to get them moving. As they did this, the rest of Symon's group, who had sneakily advanced from another area, began to fire missiles at the tanks and successfully destroyed them.

Meanwhile, Symon had crawled into the hollow base of a giant old tree and was keeping very still and quiet as a group of the attacking soldiers carefully walked through the area looking for anyone who had shot at them. They knew that they couldn't go back to the tanks so had decided to look for anyone whom they might take prisoner and use for potential bargaining later if they couldn't safely escape from the area.

Symon suddenly heard a voice which seemed to come from within himself. "You have bravely done what you could to help turn things around, and now it is time for you to leave and let others finish the task. The turning point that is taking place at this very moment could not have happened if it wasn't for your sacrifice. Know that your purpose has been achieved and that you can move on now and be free once again." Symon then heard soldiers approaching the tree where he was hiding. He jumped out from the base of the tree and started firing his gun into the air over the heads of the men who all fired back and shot him.

As Symon left his body, he suddenly became aware of the presence of Old Soul who said, "Well, my friend, we meet again. What a sacrifice you have made in this short life. At the moment, you can't even imagine what changes this sacrifice will make possible. Would you like a future glimpse of a few things that happen next?"

"I'd love that," replied Symon.

As he looked down, Symon was amazed at some of the things he observed. He saw the battle in which he had just died come to an end, and the attacking soldiers actually surrendered and defected to the side which they had been attacking. They confessed that they hadn't really wanted to carry out the attack, but their leader had given them no choice. They also shared the fact that they knew a lot of other soldiers who felt just as they did, and they didn't think their leader would remain in his position for very much longer. The captured soldiers then asked if they could now help defend the people they had been attacking!

Next Symon was shown a group of world leaders getting together to condemn the attacker and to ask that no country continue to do any kind of business with this man, not even in the area of providing food. And these leaders proclaimed that the attacking leader was guilty of war crimes and that he should be tried in an international court for his deeds.

And lastly, Symon saw Anton. First, he observed him returning to his studies, and next he saw Anton getting married. Then Symon saw Anton and his wife at the doctor's office being informed that they were going to become parents!

"Thank you, Old Soul, for making it possible for me to see such uplifting views of the future. And now I would like to go back and have a little visit with some people I have left behind." And with that, Little Soul's spirit returned briefly to Earth.

Anton was standing next to Symon's parents at his funeral. Symon gave a hug of energy to both his mother and his father. Daniela and Vadim looked at each other in amazement, hugged each other and then wept. Then Symon whispered into Anton's ear, "I look forward to seeing you again in the future, my brother. Know that you are never forgotten and I appreciate all the wonderful things you did for me while I was on this Earth."

Anton was amazed, and tears welled up in his eyes as memories of his beloved friend filled his heart. He felt so fortunate to have known Symon. He wondered what the future would hold for him now that his best friend was gone.

Another Life

Little Soul returned to his Home in the Light of the Creator and was greeted by many other Souls.

"What will you do next, Little Soul?" they all asked.

"Well, believe it or not, I want to return to Earth again," replied Little Soul. "I can't wait to get back to see some more positive changes. I've even chosen my parents! I'm sure I will have many wonderful things to share with all of you on my next return. Goodbye for now!" Then, after spending a bit more time with Old Soul, Little Soul departed for his next journey to Earth.

Little Soul arrived at the hospital where Anton and his wife, Ivanna, were preparing for the birth of their first child. He couldn't wait to be born upon this Earth again!

Anton was standing next to Ivanna as she was about to give birth. "Let's have one more big push," said the midwife. Ivanna pushed with all her strength and out popped a tiny baby boy. The midwife cleaned the baby and handed him to Ivanna who shed tears of joy. Anton also shed a few tears as he gazed lovingly into the eyes of his son, who for some reason seemed to feel familiar to Anton.

"Have you thought of a name for you son?" asked the midwife.

"Not yet," replied Anton, "but, if it's OK with you, Ivanna, I'd like to call him Symon."

"Symon, it is," replied Ivanna, and they both smiled as they looked into the eyes of their new son, who seemed to smile back at them before falling asleep.

While little Symon slept, Old Soul came for a visit. "Well, Little Soul, you have been given the name Symon yet again. I look forward to observing your efforts in this lifetime and, as always, feel free to call upon me if you require any assistance. Meanwhile, enjoy your experiences on this beautiful evolving Earth."

"I can hardly wait!" exclaimed Symon. And he continued to sleep, dreaming of things he might do this time around. "Yes, there is so much hope for this Earth!" he joyfully thought in his dreams. "What an exciting time to be here!"

--The End—